For my dad, Big Brave Ken, who isn't afraid of anything,
apart from my mum, Little Belligerent Olive.

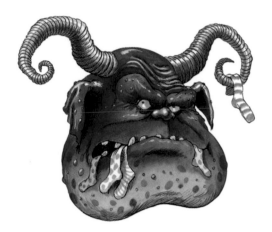

First published in Great Britain and in the USA in 2007 by
Frances Lincoln Children's Books, 4 Torriano Mews,
Torriano Avenue, London NW5 2RZ

www.franceslincoln.com

Distributed in the USA by Publishers Group West

British Library Cataloguing in Publication Data available on request

ISBN: 978-1-84507-559-0

The illustrations in this book are watercolour and black pen

Set in HooskerDont and SpookyOne

Printed in Singapore

1 3 5 7 9 8 6 4 2

You can find out more about the books by M.P. Robertson
on his website: www.mprobertson.co.uk

BIG BRAVE BRIAN

M.P. Robertson

F

FRANCES LINCOLN
CHILDREN'S BOOKS

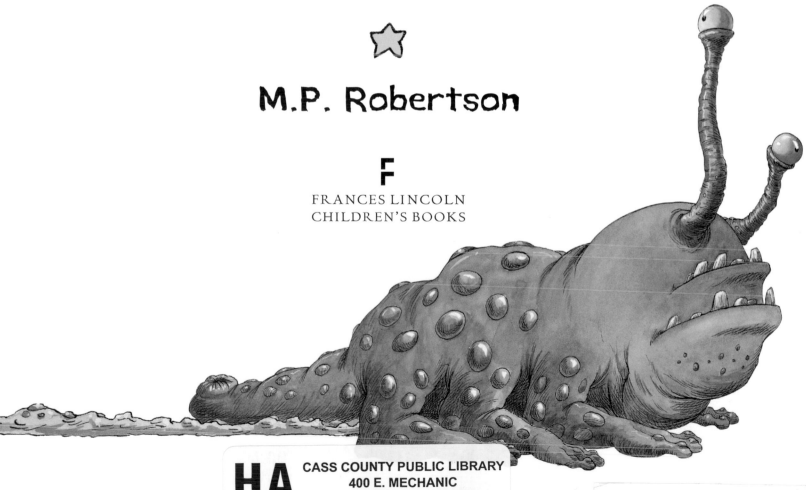

Big Brave Brian
is the bravest man in the world.

Grumpy Grizzly Bears

that live beneath the stairs
are no match for Big Brave Brian.

Big Brave Brian is not afraid of

Bottom-Biting Bog Monsters

that terrorize the toilet.

Incy Wincy Spiders

Slime-Slurpin' Slug Creatures

that drink his bathwater like soup hold no fear for Brian.

Ghastly Gawping Giants

that stare through his bedroom window don't make Brian's knees knock.

that tumble from the toy chest

don't give Brian the collywobbles.

Things that go **Bump** in the **Night**

don't give Brian the heebie-jeebies.

Sock-Munching Demons
that lurk under the bed
don't scare Big Brave Brian.

But there is one thing that even

Big Brave Brian

is scared of...